Th
Mys
Guest

Karen King

Scripture Union
130 City Road, London EC1V 2NJ.

By the same author
Topsy Turvy World – a Tiger Book

First published 1993

ISBN 0 86201 843 9

British Library Cataloguing-in-Publication Data.
A catalogue record for this book is available from the British Library.

Phototypeset by Intype, London
Printed and bound in Great Britain by Cox and Wyman Ltd, Reading

Make your own adventure

This book lets you be the writer. You can decide what happens to Charlie when she visits her cousins in Australia. You will be asked to make a choice at various stages throughout this book. After you have made a choice, follow the instructions to see what page to turn to next. Your choices will decide what happens to Charlie and her cousins. You will be responsible for the adventures they will have. Do they find out who the mystery guest is, unravel the secret message, help capture the smugglers or get trapped on the treacherous cliffs? It's up to you. So think carefully before you decide.

But don't worry if you make a wrong choice. The really exciting thing about this book is that there is not just one adventure, but seventeen of them. So you can always turn back and try again. Each choice leads you into a completely different adventure.

Have fun!

'Keep with me, I don't want you getting lost in this crowd,' Dad said, holding Charlie's hand firmly. 'And keep your eyes peeled for Uncle Peter and Aunt Carol.'

Charlie's eyes sparkled with excitement as she looked around Sydney's crowded airport. She could hardly believe it when Dad had told her that he had to go on a business trip to Australia so they would be spending two weeks with his brother and family who lived over there. She had never met her aunt, uncle or twin cousins before but she had seen several photos so was sure she would recognise them.

However, Uncle Peter found them first.

'Ken! It's great to see you!' he boomed, slapping Dad on the back.

'Peter!' Dad hugged him back, then bent to kiss the blonde woman by his side. 'You're looking well, Carol!'

'So are you, Ken,' she smiled. 'It's nice to see you again. It's been a long time.' She turned to give Charlie a hug. 'So this is Charlotte.'

Charlie shot Dad a pleading look and he grinned.

'She likes to be called Charlie. I'm afraid she's a bit of a tomboy.'

'In that case she should get on well with Justin and Gemma here,' smiled Uncle Peter. 'They're a right pair of tearaways!'

The twins grimaced at this remark.

Turn to next page.

'Ignore him, we're little angels,' Justin told Charlie.

'Most of the time, anyway,' Gemma grinned. 'Is this the first time you've been to Australia, Charlie?'

'It's the first time I've been anywhere!' Charlie sounded as excited as she felt. She still couldn't believe it was all happening. To think she was actually on the other side of the world!

'Well, you'll love it here,' Gemma said. 'We've got heaps to show you.'

'Great, I can't wait to see everything,' Charlie smiled. 'Especially a kangaroo!'

Uncle Peter laughed. 'A kangaroo's usually the first thing everyone wants to see when they come to Australia!'

Laughing and chattering, they all climbed into Uncle Peter's car.

Charlie was thrilled to discover that Uncle Peter and Aunt Carol lived in a bungalow not far from the beach. She was even more delighted to see a big swimming pool in the back garden.

'This is brilliant!' she exclaimed, looking enviously at the cool, inviting pool. A swim was just what she needed. After all that travelling, she felt hot and sticky.

Aunt Carol must have guessed what Charlie was thinking. 'Why don't you kids have a swim while I get tea ready?' she suggested. 'In fact, we'll eat out here if you like. We could have a barbecue.'

'Yes, please!' Charlie nodded eagerly. Back at home in England they'd be huddled in front of the fire now, trying to keep warm, and here they were having a swim and a barbecue in the back garden!

Turn to next page.

They sat around the pool talking until late into the evening, catching up on all the news and gossip. It was almost midnight when Charlie finally went to bed and she was exhausted. She crawled into the spare bed in Gemma's bedroom, her eyes closing as soon as she hit the pillow. As she drifted into sleep, she suddenly remembered that she hadn't said her prayers. Still, God wouldn't mind for one night . . .

'Hey, come on lazybones,' Gemma called, playfully shaking Charlie awake. 'It's almost lunch-time!'

It couldn't be morning already! Charlie was awake in an instant. 'Coming!' she said, jumping out of bed. She didn't want to miss a minute of this super holiday.

'Your dad and Uncle Peter have already gone to work,' Aunt Carol said when Charlie walked into the kitchen. 'I hope you don't mind, but I thought you would be exhausted after your long flight so I left you to lie in for a while.'

'You're right, I was whacked!' Charlie smiled at her. She felt at ease with her aunt and cousins already.

'What shall we do today?' asked Justin when Charlie had finished her breakfast. 'D'you fancy going to the beach, Charlie?'

'Or would you prefer to go to the leisure centre at the hotel and have a game of squash?' asked Gemma.

If you think they should go to the leisure centre, turn to page 14.

If you think they should go to the beach, turn to page 22.

'That's no use, we want the cops to catch them in the act,' said Justin. I'll sneak over and untie the boat and you can go back for help, Stavros. The girls can keep watch from behind the rocks.'

'That's right, keep us out of all the action!' Gemma snorted in disgust. 'Why can't one of *us* untie the boat?'

'Cos you're girls, you'd be useless,' Justin told her.

Gemma glared at her twin angrily. 'Is that so? Well, I'm going to untie that boat, Justin Baxter, and you just try and stop me!' She was so angry that she completely forgot she hadn't agreed with the idea of untying the boat anyway.

If you think Gemma should untie the boat, turn to page 64.
If you think Justin should untie the boat, turn to page 60.

She had to take the chance, it was their only way of escape. Charlie quickly pushed past the woman and darted across the room towards the door.

'Stop her, you stupid fool!' the man growled. He was still holding Justin's arm but now he lunged for Gemma too, grabbing her wrist to make sure she didn't follow Charlie.

The woman was already hot on Charlie's heels. Charlie lunged for the door handle and turned it. Relief flooded through her when she found it unlocked. She pulled open the door just as the woman grabbed her shoulder.

'Help!' she screamed at the top of her voice. 'Luigi! Help! The cleaners are really thieves!'

Luigi had been waiting in the corridor, peering around the wall, waiting anxiously for a sign of his friends. As soon as he heard Charlie shouting he ran out to see what was going on.

Realising their game was up, the two thieves released their hold on Justin and Gemma and made a dash for it. As they ran down the corridor, Justin pushed the laundry trolley after them. It hurtled down the corridor and crashed into the thieves, knocking them over just as the Mystery Man and another guest stepped out of the lift.

'Stop them! They're thieves!' the children shouted.

Turn to page 24.

'Oh, Stavros had it for an early birthday present,' Justin quickly lied. 'He said I could borrow it.'

'Yeah and sorry about dinner, Mum, but Mr Pendle let us have a pizza for helping him out in the diner. You know how busy he gets this time of year,' Gemma quickly butted in.

Charlie bit her lip and hurried into the bedroom to change before Dad came home from work and noticed the new top she was wearing. It was silly of them not to realise that their parents would notice that they had more money to spend. They'd have to be more careful in future if they wanted to avoid more awkward questions.

That night Charlie prayed, 'Please don't let us get into trouble, Jesus. After all we didn't really steal the money, we found it. So it can't really be wrong, can it?'

The next week went all too quickly. Telling their parents that they were spending the day at the beach or leisure centre, they all went off to the cinema, amusement park or wherever else they fancied. At first Charlie felt terrible about lying but it got easier after a while and before long she didn't think twice about it, she was enjoying herself so much.

'It's a shame you're going home this weekend, Ken,' Uncle Peter said on Thursday evening. 'We've really enjoyed having you and Charlie here.'

Dad smiled. 'Actually, I was thinking of staying another week. Now I've finished my business Charlie and I can do a bit of sightseeing together.'

'Oh Dad, that'll be ace!' Charlie hugged him in delight.

Suddenly there was a knock on the door.

Turn to page 82.

'Maybe. But let's take a look anyway,' Gemma said. 'What have we got to lose?'

The others agreed. Picking up their gear, they all raced along the beach.

'How much further?' gasped Charlie. 'I've got a stitch!' Her cousins and Stavros seemed to be still running with ease. But then, they were probably used to running long distances along the beach, whereas the furthest she usually ran was the corner shop and back – and that wasn't very often!

'There it is!' Justin pointed to the old surf hut just a few yards to their right, set back against the sandy bank. 'Come on! We've only got eight minutes left!'

Gemma reached the hut first. She looked around, spotted the big rock to the right and hurried over to look behind it.

'Hey, look at this!' she exclaimed, dragging a big black leather briefcase from behind the rock. 'The secret message must have been for real!'

The others had all reached the rock now and were staring at the briefcase. 'My dad takes a briefcase like that to work,' Charlie said. 'He keeps his papers and things in it.'

'Maybe there are some secret papers in here.' Justin fiddled around with the lock fastening the thick leather strap over the top of the bag, but it wouldn't budge. 'Just our luck, it's locked!' he said disappointedly.

Turn to next page.

''Course it is, stupid! They wouldn't leave it unlocked for anyone to look inside, would they?' snorted Gemma. 'The other secret agent probably has the key.'

Stavros suddenly remembered the time. He glanced at his watch and gasped – only three minutes to twelve! The other spy would be here any minute! 'Quick, let's get going before someone comes!' he hissed, glancing nervously over his shoulder. 'What if a gang of spies turns up?'

'What about this bag?' Gemma was still fiddling with the lock.

'I suppose we'd better leave it here,' said Charlie. 'It isn't ours.'

'We can't do that!' protested Justin. 'If that secret message *was* from a spy there could be top secret information in this bag. We've got to take it home with us so we can open it and find out!'

If you think they should leave the bag where it is, turn to page 49.

If you think they should take the bag home and open it, turn to page 62.

'Please, Jesus, help me,' Gemma prayed, balancing precariously on the narrow ledge, her hands clutching at a small piece of jutting rock.

Justin looked anxiously down at his sister. How long could she hold on? Then he saw her eyes closed and her lips moving. She was praying! Maybe, they should have taken Charlie's advice and prayed together before they started climbing. But it was too late now. Or was it? Maybe God would still listen and help them.

Stavros and Charlie were praying too. They knew that the only one who could help them now was God. There was no way they could survive on the cliff through the night.

It seemed like hours afterwards that they heard something overhead. At first, Justin thought it was just the wind. But the sound was getting louder and closer. He looked up and yelled to the others when he saw the helicopter hovering above. He knew it was searching for them. Soon they would be safe.

The End

'I'd like to go to the leisure centre first. I fancy a game of squash,' Charlie decided. 'Is it very far away?'

'About ten minutes' walk,' Gemma told her. 'It's in the hotel complex. Our friend Luigi's parents are managers of the Century Hotel so they let us use the leisure centre whenever we want.'

'Sounds great!' said Charlie. 'D'you think they'll let me have a look around?'

'Sure,' Justin told her. 'We'll call in the hotel for Luigi before we play squash and he'll give you a guided tour.'

As they walked into the hotel complex, Gemma grinned at the look of surprise on Charlie's face.

'Massive, isn't it?' she said. 'Wait until you see inside the hotel, it's really posh!'

An Italian lad ran to meet them as they stepped through the automatic doors into the hotel foyer.

'That's Luigi,' said Justin, waving to his friend. 'G'day, this is our cousin Charlie from England,' he said as Luigi joined them. 'We've promised to show her around the hotel – if that's OK? And then we were going to have a game of squash. D'you fancy joining us?'

Turn to next page.

'G'day!' Luigi nodded briefly at Charlie then turned anxiously to Justin. 'Can we do that later?' he asked. 'We've got this really weird guest staying at the hotel and I wanted you to take a look at him.'

'So what's new?' laughed Gemma. 'You've had loads of weird guests here. Actually, I reckon you have to be weird to stay here!'

Luigi wasn't amused. 'Very funny! This is serious, Gem. This guy is up to something, I know he is! I've just phoned to ask you to come over and your mum said you were on your way.'

Justin looked curiously at his friend. A big hotel like the Century, in a prime position about midway between the town and the beach always attracted lots of guests, and many of them were a bit weird. Eccentric, Luigi's dad called them. Luigi had often amused them with accounts of what one of the guests had got up to, but he had never phoned them at home to come over and see a guest before. This sounded serious.

'Tell us about it,' he said.

They all listened intently as Luigi explained that a mystery guest had checked in a couple of days ago. 'He calls himself Greg Simmers and he acts really weird,' he said. 'I'm sure he's wearing a disguise. And there are two other men staying at the hotel too. He pretends not to know them but I've seen them talking to each other.'

Turn to next page.

'What makes you think he's wearing a disguise?' asked Gemma.

'Well, he's wearing a wig for a start,' Luigi told her. 'He walked past me this morning and I noticed it had slipped back off his forehead a bit and a few strands of brown hair were showing.'

They all agreed *that* did sound weird. Whoever heard of a guy wearing a wig?

'Maybe he's a thief, staking out the hotel,' suggested Justin. 'I read in the paper about a gang of jewel thieves that were staying at different hotels and robbing the guests.'

'That's what I was thinking,' Luigi nodded. 'The two men he keeps meeting could be his accomplices!' He looked anxiously at his friends. 'We're holding a big party here on Friday night and that would mean lots of easy pickings for a jewel thief! Do you think we should tell my parents?'

Justin shook his head. 'They'd never believe you unless you've got proof. You know what the "oldies" are like!' He frowned and then grinned. 'I've got an idea. Let's wait until he goes out then you can sneak the key to his room, Luigi, and we'll search it. If he is a jewel thief we're bound to find some proof. Then we can tell your parents.'

Turn to page 34.

'Well, well, what have we got here! A bunch of snooping kids!' The woman grabbed Charlie by the arm and pulled her out of the wardrobe. 'Come on, out of there, all of you!'

Justin and Gemma nervously stepped out to join Charlie. A tall, fair-haired man, also dressed in a Supakleen overall, was in the process of searching through a chest of drawers. Judging by the state of the rest of the room, they had both been searching it very thoroughly. They weren't cleaners, they were thieves!

The man glared at the children and angrily strode over to the wardrobe.

'Just what we need!' he growled. 'A bunch of perishing sticky beaks!'

'What are we going to do with them?' The woman seemed really worried and nervous.

'I dunno, but one thing's for certain, we can't leave them here to go blabbing about us!' The man grabbed Justin by the arm and pulled him towards him. 'I dunno what you kids are doing here but by the time I've finished with you you'll wish you'd never set eyes on this room!' he snarled.

Charlie looked at her cousins. She could see they were every bit as terrified as she was. These people were obviously very dangerous. There was no telling what they would do. They had to escape, somehow.

Turn to next page.

The only thing she could think of was to make a dash for the door. Luigi was waiting outside for them, probably hiding somewhere. If she could get out she could shout to him to raise the alarm. The trouble was, she didn't know if the door was locked or not. If she made a run for it and the door *was* locked the thieves would be even more angry with them.

She glanced furtively over at the door. It was firmly shut. She remembered that Justin had locked it when they came into the room, so the thieves must have had a key to let themselves in. But had they locked the door after them?

If you think Charlie should dash for the door, turn to page 9.

If you think she shouldn't risk it, turn to page 46.

Down in the basement, Charlie, Gemma and Justin sat with their backs together, still bound and gagged. The thieves had escaped with their loot long ago.

They knew Luigi would be wondering what had happened to them. After a while he would get worried and confess to his parents what had happened. Then they would start looking for them. Sooner or later, someone was sure to think of looking in the basement. At least, they hoped they would . . .

The End

If you want to find out who the Mystery Man is and what he is doing at the hotel, turn to page 18 and make another choice.

The others agreed that it was best if they searched the man's room. As Luigi said, they had to find out if the man was a thief – and fast!

Luigi hurried off to get the key to the man's room while the rest of the gang went over to call the lift. It was already in use, so they pressed the button and waited, impatiently. Luigi joined them just as the lift doors opened.

Luckily, they were the only ones using the lift. Luigi pressed the button for the sixth floor and the doors glided shut. 'I don't reckon the guy will be back for ages yet,' he said. 'But one of us had better stand guard outside the room, just in case.'

They discussed it amongst themselves and agreed that Gemma, Charlie and Justin should search the room while Luigi stood guard outside. As Gemma pointed out, no one would think it was suspicious if they saw Luigi hanging about in the corridor.

As soon as the lift stopped, they stepped out and ran along the carpeted corridor.

'This is it.' Luigi stopped outside room number 56, took a key out of his pocket and unlocked it. 'Now hurry up, and don't make a mess. We don't want the guy to know someone's been in his room.'

Turn to next page.

He pushed the door open and took out the key, handing it to Justin. 'And remember to lock the door behind you. If the guy does come back he'll be suspicious if he finds the room open.'

'Will do,' nodded Justin.

'What's the danger signal?' asked Gemma.

Luigi thought for a moment. 'If I knock on the door there's danger but you've got time to come out,' he decided. 'But if I whistle then someone's about to come in the room so you'd better hide.'

The others nodded to show they'd understood and slipped into the room. Justin locked the door behind them.

It looked just like any other hotel room – nothing suspicious about it at all.

'What are we looking for?' asked Gemma.

'Stolen credit cards, bundles of money, jewellery, plans of hotels, anything suspicious,' Justin told her. 'And remember what Luigi said, no mess!'

Turn to page 58.

Charlie didn't need to think twice. 'The beach!' she replied eagerly.

'I was hoping you'd say that. I love it on the beach,' Gemma told her. 'Let's go and get our swimming cossies, then we'll call for Rashida. You'll like her, Charlie, she's fun.'

'Huh! Well I don't fancy spending the day surrounded by girls,' grimaced Justin. 'So I'll pop over and see if Stavros wants to join us.'

'Oh no, not Stavros the Great!' groaned Gemma. 'He thinks he's brilliant at everything and Justin gets just as unbearable when he's with him!' she whispered to Charlie.

Charlie grinned. It sounded like her cousins' friends were just as much fun as them. She was sure this was going to be a brilliant holiday!

'Be back for four o'clock,' Aunt Carol told them. 'And don't go swimming in the sea. You know how dangerous the currents are.'

'Don't worry, we won't,' Justin promised her.

Rashida was already out but Stavros joined them.

'G'day Charlie,' he smiled. 'What d'you think of Australia?'

Turn to next page.

'Brill!' grinned Charlie. 'I can hardly believe all this sunshine. We're right in the middle of winter back home and it's really cold and miserable.'

'I thought it always snowed in England at Christmas,' said Gemma. 'I'd love to see snow!'

'So would I!' agreed Justin. 'Do you go skiing often, Charlie?'

'We don't have *that* much snow and hardly ever at Christmas!' Charlie laughed. It was funny the ideas people had about other countries! She'd been expecting to find kangaroos bounding all over the place and her Australian friends evidently thought England was covered in snow all winter!

Soon they were on the beach.

Charlie slipped off her sandals and wriggled her toes in the soft golden sand. Now this was just as good as she'd imagined! 'It's beautiful!' she sighed. 'I could stay here all day!'

'Don't you want to look around a bit?' suggested Justin. 'There are some excellent old Aborigine caves further along the beach.'

If you think they should go to the caves, turn to page 42.
If you think they should stay on the beach for a while, turn to page 30.

Then everything happened at once; the men grabbed the thieves, more people came to see what the fuss was about, the police were called and finally, the thieves were led away for questioning.

Everyone crowded around Luigi, Justin, Gemma and Charlie, congratulating them for their bravery.

'Thanks to you kids, a notorious gang of hotel thieves has been busted,' the police sergeant said. 'Well done!'

The children were feeling pretty pleased with themselves. Things had been a bit tricky for a while but everything had worked out OK in the end.

'There's just one thing I'd like to know,' said the Mystery Man.

Everyone looked at him expectantly.

'Just what were you kids doing in my room in the first place?'

The End

If you want to find out who the Mystery Man is and what he is doing at the hotel, *turn to page 34* *and make another choice.*

'What is it?'

'Let me see!'

'Hey, fair go! Let's all have a look!' This last remark was from Gemma. Impatiently she pulled the briefcase towards her so she could see inside. 'Wow! Take a look at this!' she exclaimed. 'It's full of money!' She turned the bag upside down and bundles of crisp banknotes tumbled out onto the table. 'There must be thousands of dollars here!'

They all stared, riveted, at the bundles of money on the table.

Stavros scooped up a bundle of fifty dollar notes, his eyes wide with excitement. 'Where do you think it came from?'

'Probably a bank robbery!'

'The thief must have hid it here while he lay low for a while!'

'Gang of thieves you mean!'

They were all talking at once, excitedly grabbing handfuls of the money.

'I reckon this money's a pay-off for some secret information,' Justin said. 'I bet someone in the Government's a spy!'

'The question is . . . ' Gemma sounded so serious that they all turned to look at her. 'The question is,' she repeated. 'What are we going to do with the money?'

Turn to next page.

'Keep it, of course! Finders keepers!' declared Stavros, conveniently forgetting that he hadn't wanted to go to the old surf hut in the first place.

'We can't do that!' protested Charlie. 'It isn't our money. It'd be stealing!'

'Get real, we found it didn't we?' demanded Justin. 'So how can it be stealing? Anyway, for all we know it could have been lying there for years!'

'After all, we don't know who it belongs to . . .' Gemma looked longingly at the wad of notes in her hand.

'Yeah, and no one knows we've got it,' added Stavros. 'We'd be daft not to keep it!'

If you think they should keep the money, turn to page 47.
If you think they should tell their parents, turn to page 72.

They all thought about it carefully and decided to wait until the men had gone, as Stavros suggested, then search the caves.

'They're taking a lot of stuff in there,' Justin whispered as yet another crate was carried off the boat into the cave. 'They've got to be smugglers!'

Charlie was beginning to think he was right. What on earth could be in those crates if it wasn't smuggled goods?

After about an hour or so the men left.

The children waited until the boat was out of sight before climbing over the rocks and running up the beach to the cave.

'We'd better hurry, the tide is coming in fast!' Gemma said, as they waded through the shallow water.

'No worries. This won't take long,' Justin reassured her. 'We've got plenty of time.'

Charlie was the first one in the cave. She looked around eagerly, more interested in the strange markings on the walls than in the pile of wooden crates stacked right at the back in the dark shadows. Caves had always held a fascination for her.

'Come on, there's no time for exploring. We're supposed to be checking the crates,' called Gemma.

Turn to next page.

'Sorry.' Charlie turned around to see her friends trying to prise the lid off one of the crates. She ran over to help, curious to discover what was inside.

The task proved a lot more difficult than they'd thought.

'There must be something really valuable in here,' declared Justin. 'They've certainly secured it well!'

Finally, they managed to prise out the nails that held the lid, with Stavros's penknife. Then they pulled the lid back and peered inside.

They stared, speechless at the contents.

Charlie found her voice first.

'Costumes!' she exclaimed, taking a gold cloak out of the chest. 'It's full of costumes.'

'This is totally weird!' Gemma pulled out a pair of gold shoes.

'It could be some sort of cover, just to throw the police off the track. The drugs, or whatever, might be smuggled underneath the clothes.' Justin started pulling all the clothes out of the chest.

The others quickly joined him. But they soon discovered that the chest only contained clothes.

'Well, bang goes that theory,' said Gemma, staring into the empty chest.

'It seems they weren't smugglers after all,' said Charlie. 'Thank goodness we didn't call the police!'

Turn to next page.

'Yeah, we'd have looked right jerks,' agreed Justin. 'Let's put the lid back on the crate and get out of here!'

Stavros suddenly remembered the tide. He raced to the cave entrance and groaned. The sea was almost up to the entrance!

'Quick!' he yelled to the others. 'We've got to get out of here fast. The tide's come right up and we're almost blocked in!'

The others ran over to him. They stared in horror at the turbulent mass of sea flowing towards them. There was only a small patch of sand left dry in front of the cave.

'What are we going to do?' cried Gemma.

'Maybe we could swim to the rocks,' suggested Charlie hopefully. Although the rocks loomed up on either side of them in a sheer drop, they gradually gave way to the smaller mass they had climbed over to get into the cove. If they could swim over to that they could climb over the rocks and onto the safety of the beach on the other side.

Stavros shook his head, 'The current's too strong. We'll be carried out to sea!'

Justin looked up at the jagged cliffs of rock on either side of the cave. 'Then there's only one thing for it,' he said quietly. 'We'll have to climb the cliff.'

'We can't do that, it's too dangerous. We'll fall!' Gemma's voice was ragged with fear.

She's right, Charlie thought. But what else could they do?

Turn to page 33.

Charlie looked longingly at the sea. 'That'd be great but I'd like to have a paddle in the sea first, if that's OK?'

'Sure. We're allowed to paddle as long as we don't go out too far,' Gemma told her.

'Last one to the sea's a turkey!' shouted Stavros, already bounding across the golden sand, with Justin hot on his heels.

'Hey, you cheats!' protested Gemma as she and Charlie raced after them. 'We're all supposed to start off at the same time!'

They spent the next hour or so splashing about in the sea, taking care to stay close to the beach, before flopping down onto the sand to rest.

Turn to next page.

'Let's have a scavenger hunt,' suggested Stavros. 'We'll write down a list of things normally found around here and see who can find them first. Anyone got pencil and paper?'

'I might have,' Gemma picked up her beach bag and searched through it. 'Here's a pencil!'

'That's a pencil?' Stavros wrinkled his nose as she passed him the chewed stub of a pencil.

'Very funny!' Gemma was still rummaging through her bag. 'I can't find any paper.'

Charlie noticed a piece of screwed up paper by her foot. 'Maybe we could use this,' she said, picking it up. She unscrewed it and frowned. 'There's some weird writing on this, it must be a foreign language.'

'Let me see, maybe it's Greek.' Stavros took the paper off her to see if it was written in his native language. It wasn't. He studied it carefully, trying to make some sense of it then shook his head. 'Nope, can't make head or tail of it.'

The others crowded around to study the message. But none of them could understand it.

'I reckon it's a secret message!' Gemma's eyes sparkled with excitement. 'I bet a spy's dropped it!'

'Then how are we going to decipher it?' frowned Justin.

'I think I've got it!' cried Charlie. 'We've been doing codes at school. Lend me your pencil, please, Gemma.'

Turn to page 37.

The others were wondering the same thing. They all froze, hardly daring to breathe. To their relief, the man glanced quickly around then hurried on his way.

'Wow! That was close!' shuddered Charlie when the man had finally disappeared out of sight.

'You're telling me. He looked a right shifty character!' Gemma stood up, rubbed her knees and groaned. 'All that kneeling down has made me feel stiff!'

'Me too! I nearly died when the bloke stopped, I thought he'd spotted us!' Justin looked over in the direction the man had taken, wanting to make sure he had really gone. 'D'you reckon he is a spy?'

'I dunno, the whole thing's really weird. I reckon we should tell the "oldies" about it,' Stavros said.

Gemma agreed. 'Let's show the note to Mum when we get home.' She thrust the piece of paper into her beach bag. 'How about another splash in the sea now? I need to cool down!'

They all agreed with that! The tension of the last few minutes had been almost unbearable. They raced back down to the beach, all thoughts of spies and secret messages forgotten as they ran into the cool sea.

Turn to page 36.

Charlie bent her head and closed her eyes. 'Please, Jesus, help us. Show us what to do,' she said desperately.

'What are you doing, Charlie?'

'Amen.' Charlie opened her eyes and looked at her friends. 'Asking Jesus to show us what to do,' she told them.

'Praying!' They all stared at her incredulously.

Charlie nodded firmly. 'I always talk to Jesus when I'm in trouble, or sad about something. I pray when I'm happy too and to give thanks,' she added hastily, realising that it sounded as if she only prayed when she wanted something. 'I think if we all pray together, Jesus will tell us what to do to get out of here.'

'We haven't got time to waste on prayers,' retorted Justin. 'We've got to get out of here . . . fast! And the only way we can do that is climb up the cliff. So come on!'

If you think they should pray first, turn to page 38.
If you think they shouldn't waste any more time and start climbing the cliff, turn to page 57.

'Hey, hang on a minute, we can't go around searching someone's room – that's trespassing!' Gemma said. 'Anyway, even if the man is wearing a false beard and acting a bit strange there could be a simple explanation for it.'

'Why don't we keep an eye on the man for a while? If he is a thief we're bound to catch him out,' suggested Charlie.

Luigi looked a bit doubtful. 'But if he *is* a thief we need to know so we can warn the police before the party on Friday,' he pointed out anxiously. 'It'll be really bad for the hotel if guests get robbed here. Mum and Dad might even lose their jobs.' Suddenly Luigi grabbed Justin's arm. 'Don't look now, but he's just walked out of the lift!'

Naturally they all looked round.

A tall, dark-haired bearded man, wearing sunglasses and dressed in jeans and a casual jacket was walking over to the reception desk.

'Well, what do we do?' asked Justin. 'Follow him or search his room?'

If you think they should search the man's room, turn to page 20.

If you think they should just keep an eye on him for a while, turn to page 54.

If you think they shouldn't bother about the man at all, turn to page 83.

'I don't know . . . ' Gemma frowned. She turned to Luigi and quietly told him what they had heard the women say.

Luigi looked worried. 'Lots of guests go in the sea, and some of them forget about the strong currents and swim too far out from time to time,' he said. 'I'll go and see if I can find out who the man was.'

He got up from the table and walked out of the café.

A few minutes later Luigi returned. He looked really troubled.

'It *was* Mr Simmers,' he told them. 'Evidently he almost drowned. Luckily, one of the life-savers patrolling the beach spotted him and managed to rescue him.'

They were all quiet. Luigi knew they were all thinking the same as him. The man must have got into difficulties just after they left the beach.

Later that evening, they were amazed to hear a news report that Kelvin Starr, the famous pop star, was in hospital after almost drowning in the sea. His concert in Sydney this weekend had to be cancelled, as had his plans to start shooting the video for his latest release. The newsreader went on to say that Kelvin had been staying under another name at a local hotel.

As soon as the news report ended the telephone rang.

'Justin, Luigi's on the phone!' Aunt Carol shouted from the kitchen.

Justin, Gemma and Charlie looked at each other in stunned amazement. They all knew why Luigi phoned them. Kelvin Starr was their Mystery Man!

The End

It wasn't until later that afternoon that Gemma remembered the note and showed it to her mother.

'What's this?' Aunt Carol frowned. 'I can't make sense of it.'

'It's a secret message.'

'We found it on the beach.'

'Charlie deciphered it. It says go to the old surf hut at twelve. So we did!' Gemma told her.

'And saw a spy get a bag from behind the rock.'

The children were all talking at once, eager to tell what had happened.

'Hey, slow down! One at a time!' Aunt Carol told them. 'Now, what's this about a spy?'

Quickly, without too much butting in from the others, Justin explained about finding the message, going to the old surf hut and watching the man take the bag.

'He was really weird, Mum,' Gemma couldn't keep quiet any longer. 'Sort of shifty.'

'I must admit it does sound a bit suspicious,' Aunt Carol looked down at the note thoughtfully. 'I think I'll mention it to Constable Mitchell and see what he thinks.'

Constable Mitchell thought it sounded a bit suspicious too. He came around to talk to the children and take a description of the man.

'I'll hang on to this note for a while,' he told them. 'See what I can find out.'

Turn to page 68.

The others watched eagerly as Charlie made a few marks on the paper. 'See, you read down the first column then up the second, down the third and so on' she shouted triumphantly. 'It says, "Look behind the big rock to the right of the old hut at twelve noon." '

'It must mean the old surf hut further along the beach,' gasped Justin.

Gemma looked at her watch. 'It's twenty to twelve,' she said. 'Come on, if we hurry we can get there before twelve!'

'Get real! The note's probably been left by some kids playing a detective game,' retorted Stavros. 'Let's get on with the scavenger hunt.'

If you think Stavros is right, turn to page 67.
If you think they should go to the hut, turn to page 11.

'Hang on, it won't take up much time to say a prayer. And Charlie's right, we need Jesus at a time like this,' said Stavros.

Gemma and Justin nodded in agreement. They might be in a rush to get out of the cove, but the climb up the cliffs was very dangerous. Charlie was right, they'd all feel a lot better if they asked Jesus to help them.

They stepped back in the shelter of the cave for a moment, and together asked Jesus to help them.

'Well, I have to admit I do feel a lot better,' Justin said when they had finished their prayer. 'But now we really had better get going!'

They ran back out of the cave and stood at the bottom of the cliff. It towered above them, high, steep and treacherous.

'I hope we make it!' Stavros's voice shook with fear.

If only there was another way, Charlie thought desperately. But she knew they had to climb the cliff. The tide was coming in fast, and if it filled the cave they'd be in big trouble.

Then she remembered the crates. The men had stacked them at the back of the cave and left them. Surely that meant that the sea didn't come in that far? The men wouldn't stack crates of clothes in the caves if they were going to get wet, would they?

Turn to next page.

'Maybe we haven't got to climb the cliffs after all,' she said. 'I don't think the sea comes right into the cave.'

She reminded the others about the crates stored in the back of the cave. 'The men wouldn't put them there if the sea came in that far, would they?' she pointed out. 'So if we stay in the cave until the tide goes out again we should be safe.'

'But what if the sea does come into the cave . . . ' Justin was still worried. 'The men might not have known about the tide.'

'It won't come in very deep at first, so we'll have plenty of time to get out and climb the rock,' Stavros pointed out.

'But even if the sea doesn't come all the way in, we'll have to spend the night in the cave,' Gemma shivered at the thought.

The others weren't too happy about that either, but they all agreed that it was safer to wait in the cave and see how far the sea came in first. After all, they had nothing to lose and might be spared the treacherous climb up the cliff.

Turn to page 69.

Charlie, Justin, Gemma and Stavros all spent a sleepless night worrying. None of their parents had been very pleased about them spending some of the money they had found and had given them a stern lecture about it. They had all been pleased, however, that the children had told the truth as soon as Aunt Carol had questioned them about the money they had been spending, and had praised them for not lying about it.

Constable Mitchell came back the next day to say he'd found out that the money in the briefcase had been stolen from a hotel safe in Perth a few weeks ago.

'The hotel manager is so pleased that most of the money has been recovered that he's quite willing to forget about the money you kids spent,' Constable Mitchell said. 'But remember, next time you find anything you must tell your parents or hand it in to the police right away. Understand.'

Charlie and her cousins breathed a sigh of relief. They weren't going to get into trouble, after all.

'Don't worry, we will,' they promised.

The End

It was a wonderful afternoon; Charlie saw lots more kangaroos, some emus and even a platypus. She heard the funny laughter of the kookaburra and held a cuddly koala. She didn't want to leave. She was glad she'd remembered to pack her camera, so that she would have lots of photos to remind her of all the wonderful animals she'd seen.

'We'll come again before you go home,' Gemma promised her. 'You're here for two whole weeks so there's plenty of time.'

Charlie couldn't wait to see what other wonderful sights were in store for her in the days to come.

She went to bed that night exhausted, but this time she remembered to say her prayers before she went to sleep. She wanted to thank Jesus for the wonderful holiday she was having in Australia.

The End

'I'd love to!' Charlie told him, jumping up eagerly. 'I think caves are fascinating. Dad and I usually spend our holidays in Cornwall. There are lots of smugglers' caves down there and we always go exploring.'

'Sounds fun. I'd love to go to England,' Gemma said wistfully as they walked along the beach.

Charlie looked at her in surprise. Fancy wanting to go to boring old England when she lived in an exciting country like Australia!

Gemma noticed her surprise and grinned. 'I know it's great living here but you get bored with the sun and sea after a while. I'd like to go to England and see the snow and fog, and visit Buckingham Palace and Stratford-upon-Avon.'

'I'd like to go to America,' Stavros told them. 'When I'm older I'm going on a student exchange over there.'

'America would be good,' nodded Justin. 'But I'd really like to travel around Europe. When I'm older I'm going to back-pack around the world.'

Soon they were discussing the various countries they would like to visit. The more they talked about it the more they realised that they all wanted to travel everywhere!

Turn to next page.

They were so busy talking that they didn't notice how far they had walked.

'Hey, we're almost at the caves now,' Gemma noticed. 'They're just past those rocks.' She pointed to a mass of rocks in front of them that obscured the view of the rest of the beach and gradually formed into a high, steep cliff.

As they climbed over the rocks, Charlie noticed that they were entering a secluded bay. 'It looks lovely,' she shouted to Gemma and Justin who were just ahead.

Suddenly, they both ducked down. Justin turned around to Charlie and Stavros, his finger to his lips to warn them to be quiet, and beckoned to them to come on.

'Look!' he whispered, when they had joined them. He pointed down to the beach where they could see four men, dressed in jeans and tee shirts, carrying some huge wooden crates off a boat moored in the bay. Taking care to keep hidden behind the rocks, the children all watched intently as the men carried the crates into one of the caves set back on the beach.

'What do you think they're doing?' whispered Gemma.

'They look like smugglers to me,' Charlie whispered back. 'I bet they've smuggled some stuff into the country. They'll hide it in the caves until the coast is clear.'

Turn to next page.

'Smugglers!' Stavros repeated the word with relish. 'I reckon you're right. There are probably bottles of whisky in those cases. That's the sort of thing smugglers sneak in, isn't it?'

'Sometimes. Or it could be drugs.' Charlie tried to think of other things that were often smuggled into countries, but couldn't think of anything.

'Drugs!' Justin looked horrified.

'Maybe we should tell someone. The cops or something,' suggested Gemma.

'Good idea. Let's untie the boat to make sure the smugglers don't get away then we can get the cops.' Justin looked quite excited.

Charlie looked a bit worried. 'I don't know, maybe they aren't smugglers, after all.'

Stavros was a bit worried about that too. 'Tell you what, why don't we wait until the men have gone. Then we can sneak a look in the crates. That way we'll know whether to call the police or not.'

If you think they should untie the boat, turn to page 8.
If you think they should wait until the men have gone, turn to page 27.

'Get under the bed, quick!' Justin shouted.

They all dived under the huge four-poster bed and pulled the valance back down just as the door opened.

Gemma lifted up a corner of the valance and peered out. She could see a vacuum cleaner and a big laundry basket on wheels. 'It's the cleaners,' she whispered to the others.

Great! Charlie groaned silently. What if the cleaners decided to vacuum under the bed!

Gemma and Justin were thinking the same thing. They all frantically tried to think of reasonable excuses they could give if the cleaners discovered them hiding under the bed in one of the guests' rooms. None came to mind.

But to their surprise the vacuum cleaner wasn't switched on. Instead, there was a lot of banging, as if drawers and cupboards were being opened.

'There's nothing here,' a woman's voice said. 'Just a watch and a couple of pairs of cufflinks.'

'Keep looking,' said a man's voice. 'There's bound to be some money stashed somewhere. No one takes it all out with them.'

The three children gasped. They weren't cleaners. They were thieves! And to think they had been about to search this room themselves, thinking this man was a thief!

Justin lifted a corner of the valance and peered out. The man was searching through the wardrobe. Thank goodness they hadn't hid in there! But they might look under the bed soon. Then they would be in trouble!

Turn to page 59.

Charlie hesitated too long. The woman grabbed her shoulder and pushed her onto the bed beside Gemma.

'Sit there while we decide what we're gonna do with you!' she snapped.

The man was still holding Justin's arm. He pulled him over to the wardrobe, rummaged through it and pulled out some ties.

'We'll tie the little perishers up with these,' he snarled. 'That should keep them out of mischief!'

The woman nodded. 'Right you kids, get your hands behind your backs! And don't try any funny moves!'

Gemma, Justin and Charlie looked at each other nervously. They were all wishing the same thing; that they had never decided to snoop in this room. But it was too late now. Slowly they put their hands behind their backs.

A few minutes later they were all bound, gagged and thrust into the huge laundry basket.

Turn to page 71.

'I think we should tell our parents about it anyway,' Charlie said.

'Are you crazy?' scoffed Stavros. 'They'll only make us hand it over to the police and then it'll go to police funds or something!'

'Let's have a vote,' suggested Gemma. 'All those in favour of keeping the money raise their hands.'

Charlie looked at the pile of money and thought of all the things she could buy with it. Maybe the others were right. After all, they had found the money so why shouldn't they keep it? It wasn't as if they were stealing it, was it? They hadn't taken it off anyone. They didn't even know who it belonged to. Slowly she raised her hand to join the others.

'Vote carried unanimously,' declared Justin. 'We keep the money!'

Turn to page 51.

They soon found out.

Later that afternoon, Luigi's father asked them to come into his office.

They were surprised to see the Mystery Man sitting there. His wig was now firmly in place.

'Mr Simmers has been telling me how you kids raised the alarm when he got in trouble on the beach earlier on,' smiled Mr Derwent. 'I'm very pleased with you all.'

'We were glad to help.' Luigi looked over at the man. He rose from his chair and walked over to them.

'I'd like to give you something as a reward,' he said. 'But first I want your promise that you'll keep a secret.'

The children looked at him and then at Mr Derwent. He smiled and nodded.

'You've got it,' they all promised.

'Great. Well I think you've all guessed that I'm not really Mr Simmers.'

They all gaped as the Mystery Man took off his wig to reveal close-cropped, brown hair. 'The beard's dyed,' he grinned. 'But maybe you can still recognise me?'

Charlie knew immediately. She just couldn't quite believe it.

'Kelvin Starr!' she stammered.

Of course, now they all recognised him. But what was a famous pop star doing here?

Turn to page 81.

'But if there *is* top secret information in the bag, we're best to leave it where it is,' Gemma pointed out. 'If anyone finds out we've got it we could end up in major strife.'

'I guess you're right,' agreed Justin. We'd better put it back.'

He picked up the briefcase and pushed it back behind the rock.

Stavros grabbed his arm. 'Hide behind the hut, quick!' he hissed. 'Someone's coming!'

They all ducked behind the hut as a stockily built, fair haired man came into sight. The man glanced furtively over his shoulder then marched briskly up to the rock. Reaching behind it, he grabbed the briefcase and pulled it out.

The four children held their breath as the man inspected the briefcase. They wondered if he was going to open it and if so, what would be inside. But the man was merely checking that the lock hadn't been tampered with. Once certain of that he looked furtively over his shoulder again, then walked briskly past the hut.

Charlie gasped as the man walked within a few centimetres of her. To her horror he hesitated and looked around again. Her blood ran cold. Had he heard her?

Turn to page 32.

It turned out that the men belonged to a PR agency handling the publicity for Kelvin Starr, the famous pop star. The crates contained equipment and props for a video they were shooting to promote Kelvin's new album. They wanted to shoot the video early the next morning, so they were stacking the equipment in the cave overnight.

Luckily, the policeman and the PR men thought it was quite amusing that the children had thought they were smugglers.

'Never be afraid to call us if you see anything suspicious,' one of the policemen said. 'But remember, you must never take any action yourself. If the men really had been smugglers and they'd caught you untying the boat you could have found yourselves in big trouble.'

'We will,' the children promised.

Charlie knew her friends felt every bit as bad as she did. Fancy almost destroying Kelvin Starr's video! 'We're sorry,' she told the PR men. 'We didn't mean to cause you any trouble.'

The others apologised too. 'I hope we haven't messed up your plans,' Justin told them.

'Well, we've got the boat back so no harm's done,' one of the men grinned. 'Tell you what, we could do with some more background people for the video. How do you kids fancy being in it?'

'Wow! Unreal! D'you mean it?' Gemma asked eagerly. They all crowded around the men, their faces aglow with excitement.

'Fair dinkum' the man nodded. 'Be here at eight in the morning, ready for shooting. Oh – and mind you get your parents' permission first.'

The children were delighted. Especially Charlie. What a fantastic start to her holiday!

The End

They all had a great time over the next few days. With money being no object they could go wherever they liked and buy whatever they wanted. Charlie had never had so much fun.

'Well, you kids seem to be enjoying yourselves,' said Aunt Carol when they came back one afternoon. 'But I bet you're starving now! Get yourselves washed and I'll dish up dinner.'

'It's OK, Mum, we're not hungry,' said Justin. 'We've just had a pizza.'

Aunt Carol frowned. 'You had a pizza yesterday as well,' she said. 'Your pocket money seems to be stretching remarkably well this week.' Then she noticed the new skateboard that Justin was carrying. 'And where did you get that from? It looks really expensive.'

Gemma and Justine exchanged nervous glances. How were they going to explain their sudden windfall to their mother?

If you think they should tell Aunt Carol about finding the money, turn to page 78.
If you think they should make up an excuse, turn to page 10.

'It's a waste of time hanging about here and watching him have a swim,' sighed Justin. 'Let's go back to the hotel.'

Luigi shrugged his shoulders. 'Might as well. It doesn't look as if anything interesting is happening here anyway.'

'I think you might be wrong about this guy, Luigi,' Gemma said as they walked back to the hotel. 'After all, if he was wearing a wig he wouldn't go swimming in the sea, would he? It could come off!'

'Yeah, and all he had in his bag was swimming gear,' added Justin. 'I reckon we were way off course. He isn't a jewel thief at all.'

'Maybe . . . ' Luigi admitted reluctantly. 'Anyway let's forget him for a bit and show Charlie around. Would you like to see the hotel gift shop first, Charlie? There's loads of souvenirs and craft things in there. It's really interesting.'

'I'd love to,' Charlie told him. She always spent ages looking in gift shops when she and Dad were on holiday. She liked to get a souvenir from every place they visited.

The gift shop was full of souvenirs: boomerangs, Aboriginal paintings, a wide range of stationery and stickers featuring Australian wildlife, cuddly toy kangaroos, koalas – all the usual things you would expect to find in a gift shop but all the more interesting because they were Australian. Charlie was fascinated.

Turn to next page.

The others, however, had seen it all before and although they tried to be patient for Charlie's sake, after half an hour or so they started to get itchy feet.

'Hey, come on, or else there'll be no time to see the rest of the place!' Gemma reminded her. 'You'll have plenty of time to browse around here again and decide what souvenirs you're taking home.'

Charlie put down the cuddly kangaroo she'd been carefully looking at. 'Sorry. I bet you're all fed up with waiting for me,' she apologised. 'It's just there's so much to look at! I definitely want one of those kangaroos. I'd buy it today if I'd brought enough money with me!'

'Most people like those,' Luigi told her. 'So don't worry, we always keep plenty in stock. You can get one any time you want.'

After the gift shop they decided to go into the coffee bar for a milk shake.

Two women were sitting at the table next to them and they couldn't help overhearing them say something about one of the guests being taken to hospital because he had got into difficulties in the sea.

'You don't think that's the Mystery Man, do you?' Charlie whispered to Gemma.

Turn to page 35.

'It's only Monday, we've got plenty of time to keep an eye on this Mystery Man and find out what he's up to,' Gemma pointed out. 'But if we get caught searching his room we'll probably be grounded for the rest of our lives!'

The others agreed that made sense.

'Quick, stand around in a group and pretend we're discussing something,' whispered Luigi. 'We don't want him to suspect that we're following him.'

That sounded good advice so they all crowded around, pretending to chat. Luigi and Justin were both facing the reception desk, so they could see what was going on.

'I wonder what's in that bag?' Justin was staring at the large blue holdall that the man was carrying.

'Maybe his burglar tools – or some of his loot!' suggested Gemma.

They all watched intently as the Mystery Man handed his key to the receptionist and strode towards the hotel entrance. Just as she hung the keys up, the telephone rang.

'Mr Simmers!' the receptionist shouted, holding out the receiver. 'It's for you!'

The Mystery Man turned and walked back to the reception desk.

Turn to next page.

Charlie and the others huddled together again, pretending they were in earnest conversation. This time Charlie was facing the man, so she whispered reports of his actions.

'He doesn't look very pleased . . . he's finished talking now . . . he's leaving . . . '

She watched as the man hurried out of the hotel. 'You can turn around now, he's gone!'

'Come on then, we'd better get after him,' urged Luigi.

'We don't want to be too close behind, or he'll spot us,' Justin reminded him.

'Yeah, but we don't want to be too far away either or we'll lose him!' Luigi pointed out.

Gemma interrupted them, 'Look, he's left his bag behind!' she said, pointing over to the blue holdall on the floor by the reception desk. The receptionist was just walking into the office.

'That's brilliant!' gasped Justin. 'Let's sneak a look inside it before the receptionist comes back. Then we'll know for certain whether he's a thief or not.'

If you think they should sneak a look inside the bag, turn to page 80.

On the other hand, if you think they should leave the bag alone and follow the man, turn to page 93.

Constable Mitchell whistled when he saw all the money in the bag.

'You kids are old enough to know you shouldn't have kept this money. You should have reported it right away,' he said sternly. 'You should always hand anything you find over to the police so we can try and trace the real owners. If you keep it yourself, then you're stealing it. Understand?'

They all exchanged guilty glances. He was right, they had known they shouldn't have kept the money. Justin and Gemma wished they had reported it right away like Charlie had said. And Charlie wished she'd had the courage to stick up for what she'd known was right instead of going along with the others.

'Yes, sir. Sorry,' they all mumbled in unison, looking down miserably at their feet.

'What will happen now?' asked Aunt Carol.

'We'll have to question their friend . . . ' he looked in his notebook to check the name, 'Stavros. Then see if we can check out where this money came from. It's probably stolen so we should have records of it. We'll get back to you as soon as we find out anything.'

Turn to page 40.

Justin started to climb up the steep cliff. Stavros and Gemma followed close behind him.

'Come on, Charlie!' Gemma shouted over her shoulder. 'There's no time to waste!'

Charlie looked up at the high cliff and felt a shiver of fear. If only there was another way out!

Please help us, Jesus, she prayed again silently, as she followed her friends up the cliff.

The climb was treacherous. There were very few footholds to grip onto and they took every step, taut with fear, knowing that one wrong move and they would plunge down into the sea below.

'It's no good, we can't climb any higher. There's nothing to grip onto!' Justin shouted. 'We'll have to try and move across the cliff instead of up. Then maybe we can come down further along the beach.'

'I can't!' Gemma screamed. 'I can't move off this ledge!'

Justin looked down at his sister, his heart thudding when he saw that she was trapped on a narrow ledge in the middle of the high cliff. There was nothing for her to grip onto to help her move off it. Perhaps he could go back and help her. He looked to the side of him and saw only sheer cliff. He couldn't move either. They were all trapped on the cliff.

Turn to page 13.

Charlie went over to a chest of drawers, opened it then shut it again. She didn't feel comfortable looking through other people's private things. It wasn't right. She knew how she'd feel if anyone snooped through her things! She wished she'd had the courage to refuse when the others had suggested it. Still, it wasn't too late.

'I don't think we should be doing this,' she said. 'It's wrong to sneak into someone else's room and snoop around.' She took a deep breath. 'I'm going out.'

Gemma and Justin felt uneasy too. Now they were inside the room, they felt like burglars. OK, they were only looking and weren't going to steal anything, but Charlie was right. They shouldn't be doing it.

'Yeah, let's get out of here,' they agreed.

Suddenly there was an urgent knock on the door.

They all looked at each other in horror. Luigi was telling them that someone was coming!

'Does that mean we run out or hide?' whispered Gemma.

No one could remember!

If you think they should run out of the room and hope to get away, turn to page 66.

If you think they should hide in the wardrobe, turn to page 74.

If you think they should hide under the bed, turn to page 45.

Meanwhile, Luigi ran along the corridor to hide around the corner. He peered out, waiting for the door to open so he could beckon his friends to his hiding place. But they didn't come out. He watched anxiously as the cleaners came out of room 57 and pushed the huge laundry basket and vacuum cleaner into room 56. What were Gemma, Justin and Charlie doing? Why hadn't they come out of the room when he knocked on the door? There had been plenty of time for them to get away before the cleaners had come out of the next room. He'd told them if he knocked on the door it was safe to come out, but if he whistled to hide. The stupid fools must have got the signals mixed up and hid instead. Now the cleaners would find them and they'd have to confess what they were doing there. His folks would really stress out! He'd probably be put on cleaning duties until he left school to make up for this!

Suddenly the door of room 56 opened. Luigi held his breath, expecting to see the cleaners angrily frog-marching his friends out.

To his surprise, the cleaners came out alone. They locked the door behind them and pushed the laundry basket and vacuum along to the next room. The last one along this corridor.

Luigi waited impatiently. What on earth were Justin, Gemma and Charlie doing?

Turn to page 70.

'Oh no, you're not!' Justin ducked down behind the rocks and raced to the beach. Gemma glared at him angrily.

'Then I'll go for help!' she declared and was away over the rocks, heading towards the beach before any of them could stop her.

'I wish they'd stop trying to outdo each other – especially at times like this!' grumbled Stavros.

Justin peered over the rocks. Good! The men were still in the cave. All he had to do was dash over to the boat, slip the rope off the anchor and run back to the rocks for cover. It should be easy.

Casting another glance at the cave to make sure none of the men had emerged, he raced over to the boat. Quickly, he grabbed hold of the rope and pulled it over the anchor.

'Oi, what do you think you're doing?' One of the men had come out of the cave and was racing down towards him. He was a very broad, muscular man and looked extremely angry. Not the sort of man to stop and argue with. Justin dropped the rope and ran for the safety of the rocks.

Stavros and Charlie thought it best to get out of there too. They scrambled back over the rocks and ran back along the beach, closely followed by Justin. On and on they ran, until they were sure they had put a safe distance between themselves and the smugglers.

Turn to next page.

'Phew! That was a close shave!' panted Justin, throwing himself down on the sand.

Stavros and Charlie flopped down beside him. They were all out of breath. They had never run so fast in their lives!

Then Charlie remembered something, 'What about Gemma?'

A look of alarm crossed Justin's face. 'Oh no, I forgot all about Gem!' Then he smiled with relief. 'It's OK, here she is!'

Gemma was running along the beach towards them. 'What are you doing?' she shouted. 'Why aren't you waiting by the rocks?'

Briefly they told her what had happened.

'Huh! And you said I'd botch it up!' she told Justin. 'A fine mess of it you've made. I just hope the cops arrive before the smugglers get away.'

'You called them, then?' asked Justin.

'I saw Tim, he's going to call them.' Tim was the life-saver.

'What shall we do now, then?' asked Charlie.

Much as they wanted to see what was going on, none of them fancied going back to the caves.

'Let's go home,' Justin suggested. 'Tim will drop by and tell us what happened.'

They all agreed that was the best thing to do.

Turn to page 89.

'There's no time to argue!' Stavros grabbed the bag and headed for the bank behind them. 'We've got to get outta here – fast!'

They quickly scrambled over the bank and raced home, not daring to look back and see if anyone was watching them. They were all gasping for breath by the time they reached the safety of the bungalow.

'Let's go to the garage, we're sure to find something to open the bag with there,' panted Gemma.

Uncle Peter and Charlie's dad were still at work, and had taken the car with them, so the garage was unlocked. Justin opened the door and they all crowded inside.

'What can we use to open it?' asked Stavros, putting the briefcase down on the work-table along the side wall.

'We'll have to pick the lock with a nail – it's easy, I've seen it done on TV,' Justin told him. He picked up a nail and poked it about inside the lock. The others watched expectantly. But, after several attempts, he threw the nail down in exasperation. 'It's hopeless! We'll have to try something else!'

'Why don't we cut the strap instead?' suggested Gemma. 'Then we can pull the bag open.'

Turn to next page.

She searched among her father's tools, selected a sharp knife and started to cut through the thick leather strap just above the lock. It was so thick that by the time she was half-way through her fingers were feeling sore. She put the knife down and flexed her fingers. 'Ow! I'm gonna get blisters!'

'Here, I'll finish cutting it.' Justin picked up the knife and continued cutting the strap where his sister had left off.

Charlie, Stavros and Gemma watched anxiously, wondering what they would find inside the bag.

'Done it!' Justin shouted excitedly. He pulled the strap back, opened the briefcase and peered inside. His mouth dropped open in amazement as he stared, wide-eyed, at the contents of the briefcase.

Turn to page 25.

'Suit yourself,' Justin shrugged his shoulders carelessly. He knew how stubborn his sister could be and there wasn't time to stand there arguing about it. 'I'll go back and get help. You two keep watch,' he told Charlie and Stavros.

Gemma smiled in triumph as Justin climbed back over the rocks and raced along the beach. Then she turned towards the caves and frowned. Untying the boat didn't seem like a good idea now she'd won. Still, she couldn't back out now. The others would never let her live it down. The men were inside the cave so it was now or never. Taking a deep breath, she bent down and made her way towards the sea, using the rocks as cover.

Charlie and Stavros watched anxiously as Gemma peered out from the rocks, saw the men were still inside the cave and raced over to the boat. Quickly, she slipped the rope securing the boat off the anchor and raced back to the rocks for cover.

'Well done,' Stavros whispered as Gemma joined them.

Gemma smiled at the praise. She felt quite pleased with herself. The tide was coming in and already the boat was starting to drift away. Wait until Justin came back, he'd have to admit she'd done a good job then!

Charlie bit her lip as she watched the boat sailing away. What if they were wrong and the men weren't smugglers?

Turn to next page.

'You weren't long,' Stavros said as Justin clambered up the rocks to join them again.

'I saw Tim, the life-saver and told him all about it. He's calling the cops,' Justin told him.

Two of the men were coming out of the cave now, talking earnestly to each other. Suddenly one of them noticed the boat and yelled. Two others came running out of the cave and they all raced down towards the beach, shouting angrily.

The four children watched as the men waded into the water after the boat. But it had drifted too far out. One of the men dived into the water and swam after it.

'I wish the cops would hurry up!' whispered Justin. 'If he catches up with the boat they'll be able to get away!'

'Here they are!' shouted Gemma, pointing to the police boat which was speeding towards the man in the sea.

Everything happened very fast. The police hauled the man on board then headed towards the beach.

'That's funny, why haven't the smugglers tried to make a run for it?' muttered Stavros.

The others were thinking the same thing. It was very strange that the smugglers actually went up to the policemen and started talking to them. It was even stranger when they led them to the caves where they had hidden the crates.

'Maybe they're not smugglers after all,' said Charlie.

They looked at each other. It was beginning to look as if they had made a dreadful mistake.

'I think we'd better get out of here, fast!' said Justin.

'And I think you'd better stay right where you are. We've got a few questions to ask you!'

Charlie and the others looked up, right into the stern face of a policeman!

Turn to page 50.

'We can't be in immediate danger if Luigi can knock on the door,' said Justin. 'Let's get out, quick!'

He ran over to the door, opened it slowly and peered out. Luigi was pacing up and down nervously outside.

'About time!' he hissed. 'The cleaners have just gone in next door. Lock the door quick and let's get out of here before they come out and cop us!'

Justin's hands were shaking as he locked the door. As quietly as they could, they ran down the corridor, not stopping until they reached the lift.

'That was a close shave!' gasped Luigi. 'My parents would have killed me if they knew we'd been searching a guest's room.'

'We were just about to come out when you knocked on the door,' Gemma told him. 'As soon as we got in there we knew it was the wrong thing to do.'

They realised it was a close escape and decided that snooping in someone else's room wasn't such a good idea after all, no matter what the reason. They decided to forget all about the Mystery Man before they got into big trouble.

'Let's go and have a game of squash,' suggested Gemma. 'It's more fun – and safer!'

They all agreed with that.

The End

If you want to find out who the Mystery Man is, turn to page 34 and make another choice.

'He's right,' said Gemma. 'I bet some kids have planted this note. They'll be waiting to see if anyone's dumb enough to take any notice of it. They're probably watching us right now, ready to laugh themselves silly if we start running to the surf hut.'

The others agreed to ignore the note and carry on with the scavenger hunt.

'You make the list of things we've got to find,' Stavros told Charlie, 'seeing as you've got the pencil and paper.'

'Hang on, we need a list each, otherwise we'll forget what we've got to find,' Gemma reminded them. 'And we haven't got enough paper for that.'

'I hadn't thought of that,' admitted Stavros. 'Maybe a scavenger hunt isn't such a good idea, after all.'

'Hey, I've got it! Charlie wants to see a 'roo so why don't we take her to the wildlife park?' Justin looked really pleased with himself for thinking of such a brilliant idea.

'What's a 'roo? Oh, you mean kangaroo!' Charlie guessed. 'Oh yes, I'd love that. Is the park far?'

Justin shook his head. 'Just a short bus ride away. If we head off home now and get changed we can take some sandwiches and have a picnic lunch there.'

They all agreed that was a fun way to spend the afternoon.

Turn to page 84.

A couple of days later, Constable Mitchell returned to tell them that a local hotel manager had recognised the handwriting. It belonged to one of his barmen who had disappeared a couple of weeks ago, just after a gang of thieves had broken into the hotel safe and escaped with a lot of money. The police were issuing a description of the barman and the man who had picked up the bag, so that they could question them in connection with the robbery.

'You did well to mention this, kids,' smiled Constable Mitchell. 'We've been trying to bust this gang for months and now, thanks to you, we might have got a lead on them.'

The following evening, there was an announcement on the news that a gang of thieves who had been working hotels throughout the country had been busted by the police. Charlie and her cousins smiled at each other, pleased that they had been able to help.

The End

Charlie was right, the sea didn't come right up to the cave. A little trickled into the entrance, but that was it, the rest of the cave remained dry.

And, as it turned out, they didn't have to spend the night in the cave, waiting for the tide to go out again. Aunt Carol got so worried when none of the children returned home at four o'clock, as she'd told them, that she contacted the life-saver. He searched the beach, found their bags where they'd left them by the rocks and guessed they were trapped in the cave, so got the lifeboat out to rescue them.

When they were all safely tucked up in their beds that night, the four children said a prayer of thanks to Jesus for helping them get home safely.

The End

If you want to know what the crates were doing in the cave, turn to page 44 and make another choice.

'They've gone!' Justin scrambled out from under the bed, closely followed by Charlie and Gemma.

'Thank goodness for that, I thought I was going to sneeze . . . atchoo!' The sneeze Charlie had been trying to hold back for the past five minutes finally erupted.

'So those cleaners are the thieves! And just look at the mess they've made!' said Gemma.

The thieves had pulled out the contents of the drawers, cupboards and wardrobes, leaving them scattered all over the floor.

'We'd better go and tell someone!' said Justin. 'We can't let them get away with this!'

'But how are we going to explain what *we* were doing in the room?' Gemma reminded him.

Luigi was very relieved to see his friends were safe.

'What's going on?' he hissed. 'Did you find anything?'

Justin quickly told him what had happened.

'What! We'd better raise the alarm quick!' Luigi was already racing along the corridor to the lift.

'Hang on!' puffed Justin when they'd caught up with him. 'How are we going to say we found out?'

That was the million dollar question. They were all silent as the lift took them down to the ground floor.

Finally Charlie spoke up. 'We'll have to tell the truth.'

They all knew she was right. Telling the truth was the only way to catch the thieves.

'I guess we'll be in major strife now,' sighed Gemma. 'But we did wrong so we'll just have to wear it.'

Turn to page 77.

Luigi was very puzzled to see the cleaners come out of the room, pushing the laundry trolley, with still no sign of his friends. Justin and the others must have found a good hiding place, he thought.

The cleaners seemed in a real hurry. They locked the door but instead of going into the next room to clean that, they hurried on right down the corridor to the lift instead. Luigi waited until they were out of sight, then ran up to room 56. He knocked on the door.

'Come on, it's safe to come out now!' he shouted as loud as he dared.

He waited for a minute but there was no answer. So he turned the handle of the door. Of course, the cleaners had locked it! Luigi reached in his pocket for the key then remembered that he'd given it to Justin. He knocked on the door again, louder this time. There was still no answer. What on earth was going on? What had happened to Justin, Gemma and Charlie?

Turn to page 19.

'Charlie's right,' Justin agreed reluctantly. 'We can't keep this money. It would be wrong, and we know it.'

They all nodded rather unenthusiastically. Much as they all wanted to keep the money, they knew it was wrong.

'We'd better go and tell Mum about it. She'll know what to do,' Gemma sighed, putting the bundle of money she was holding back in the briefcase.

The others followed suit. Then, they scooped the pile of notes off the table into the bag. When all the money had been put back, they went to find Aunt Carol.

She was out in the back garden, weeding.

'G'day,' she smiled as they approached her. 'I didn't expect you back so early. Did you enjoy yourselves on the beach?' Then she noticed the black briefcase Justin was carrying in his arms. 'What have you got there?'

'We found it on the beach,' Justin put the briefcase down beside his mother. 'That's why we came back early.'

Aunt Carol frowned. 'A briefcase? What on earth was it doing on the beach?'

'It was by the old surf hut,' Gemma told her.

'It's full of money,' Charlie burst out.

'Thousands and thousands of dollars!'

'Millions you mean!'

Turn to next page.

'Look!' Justin opened the bag, thrust his hand inside and pulled out a bundle of banknotes.

Aunt Carol looked as if she was going to faint. She stared speechlessly at the money for a moment, then put down the fork and took off her gardening gloves. Slowly, she reached out and touched the money, as if testing whether it was real. She took the bundle off Justin, examined the notes, then counted them.

'Are they all fifty dollar notes?' she asked.

'Most of them,' said Justin. 'There's a couple of bundles of a hundred dollars.'

'I see. Well, I think I'd better take care of that bag,' Aunt Carol got up off her knees and took the briefcase from Justin. 'Now, come inside and tell me where you found it.'

Aunt Carol listened attentively whilst they explained about finding the note on the beach, which led them to the bag hidden by the old surf hut.

'You could have got yourselves into a very dangerous situation there,' she told them. 'I'm sure this money has been stolen. Probably from a bank raid or something. If the thieves had come along and seen you with the bag they would have been very angry. Who knows what could have happened!'

The four children exchanged worried looks. They hadn't thought of that. Suddenly they felt very nervous.

Turn to page 87.

'Quick, hide in the wardrobe!' hissed Gemma. 'It's big enough for us all to cram in!'

They all raced over to the fitted wardrobe that covered one wall in the bedroom, jumped in and shut the doors just as the bedroom door opened.

The wardrobe was crammed with clothes. It was pitch black inside and terribly stuffy. Charlie prayed that they wouldn't have to stay in there for long. She couldn't stand it. She knew her friends were probably feeling the same.

They all strained their ears and listened intently. They could hear the low murmur of voices and some banging. What was going on? No one dared speak but they were all thinking the same thing. What if the Mystery Man opened the wardrobe?

The stuffy darkness was suddenly enveloped in a shaft of light as the wardrobe doors were flung open. But instead of the bearded Mystery Man standing there, they were astonished to see a thin, middle-aged woman with her dark hair tied back in a headscarf and dressed in a blue overall bearing the motif Supakleen. It was the cleaners!

Turn to page 17.

'So do I,' agreed Dad. 'I've enjoyed myself too. Australia is a wonderful country and you've all made us really welcome. But this was a *business* trip.'

Luigi's parents looked at each other and smiled. 'Well, there is one person who would like to meet you before you go back,' she said. 'In fact he particularly wants to meet all you youngsters.'

'Us?' Justin, Gemma and Charlie looked at Luigi in surprise. 'Who is he?'

Luigi's grin was so wide it almost stretched from ear to ear. 'Wait and see!'

'Ah, this must be him now,' Luigi's mother smiled as she got up to answer the knock on the door.

They were all amazed to see that their surprise guest was the Mystery Man who had been staying at Luigi's hotel.

'I forgot all about him,' whispered Gemma. 'I wonder why he wants to meet us.'

They were even more amazed when Mr Simmers took off his wig to reveal short, closely-cropped brown hair.

'The beard's dyed,' he grinned. 'Anyone recognise me?'

The deep, husky voice with its English accent, and the close-cropped hair were a dead giveaway!

'Kelvin Starr!' they all screamed. It was unbelievable. They were actually talking to their favourite pop star!

Turn to next page.

Kelvin grinned. 'I hear you kids all thought I was a jewel thief!'

So they had! Thank goodness they hadn't done anything stupid like searched his room!

'Mum and Dad introduced me to him yesterday,' smiled Luigi. 'I knew you'd like to meet him as well!'

Kelvin explained that he was staying at the hotel because he wanted to make a video for his new song release. He was in disguise because he didn't want to be bombarded by fans. He gave the four friends his autograph and posed with them while Luigi's parents took some photographs. They were all thrilled.

Early next morning, Charlie and her father set off for home. Aunt Carol, Uncle Peter, Gemma and Justin came to see them off.

'We'll miss you,' they told Charlie. 'Don't forget to write to us.'

'I won't,' she promised.

As she looked out of the window of the plane she remembered how excited she had been about going to Australia. Well, her holiday was even better than she'd hoped. Although she was a bit sad about leaving, she couldn't wait to get back home and tell her friends what a wonderful time she'd had. Especially about meeting Kelvin Starr!

The End

The two bogus cleaners were very surprised to find the police waiting for them when they tried to leave the hotel with their loot. It turned out that they were part of a team working the hotels throughout New South Wales. The police were pretty confident that they would spill the beans about the other gang members.

'Well done, kids!' the police sergeant said. 'We've been trying to bust this gang for a while now. Thanks to you four, we'll soon have them safely behind bars!'

The four children all had a good talking to from their parents, and they promised they would never, ever snoop in someone's room again. Everyone agreed that they must have had a real fright when the thieves were in the room, and were very pleased that they had raised the alarm and told the truth about what they were doing in the room. So they all agreed not to punish them – this time!

'Don't worry, there'll never be a next time!' the children promised.

The End

'Well, I'm waiting,' Aunt Carol said firmly, her grey eyes sweeping over them. 'Where have you been getting all this money from?'

'We . . . er . . . found it.' Justin shuffled his feet uneasily and dropped his gaze.

'Where? And how much did you find?'

'It was hidden by the old surf hut,' Gemma told her. 'There was a whole bagful of money. Millions of dollars!'

'We haven't spent it all,' Justin added hastily. 'We've still got lots left.'

Aunt Carol raised her eyebrows questioningly. 'Really? Well I think you'd better show me this money and tell me exactly how you found it.'

Justin ran to fetch the bag of money from where they had hidden it. Meanwhile, Gemma and Charlie told Aunt Carol all about finding the note on the beach, then going to the surf hut and finding the bag of money behind the rock.

They had just finished as Justin came back with the briefcase. He put it on the table and opened it up. Aunt Carol's eyes almost popped out of her head when she saw the bundles of crisp banknotes packed inside it.

Turn to next page.

She reached out and haltingly picked up a bundle of notes, staring incredulously at it. Then, she raised her eyes slowly to look at the three children in front of her. 'You were going to keep all this?' she stammered.

'Well we did find it!' Gemma said defensively.

'Yeah, and we didn't know whose it was so finders keepers.' Justin's voice faltered as if he didn't sound too confident.

Charlie could see that her aunt was very annoyed.

'I guess we should have told you straight away really,' she said. 'Sorry, Aunt Carol.'

'You certainly should have told me right away,' Aunt Carol said sternly. 'You all know very well that it was wrong to keep this money. However, I am pleased that you've told me the truth now.'

'What are you going to do?' asked Gemma as Aunt Carol picked up the phone.

'I'm ringing Constable Mitchell, of course,' she said. 'He'll know what to do about this.'

'That's the local bobby,' whispered Gemma, looking rather pale. 'Now we're done for!'

Charlie bit her lip nervously as she watched her aunt dial the policeman's number. She knew Gemma was right and they were all going to be in big trouble for spending some of the money they had found.

Turn to page 56.

They ran over to the desk and Luigi grabbed the bag. 'Keep a look out, make sure no one's coming!' he said.

Justin watched the door while Charlie looked anxiously over at the office hoping the receptionist wouldn't come out. She didn't feel comfortable about this at all. She knew it was wrong to sneak a look in someone else's bag but she didn't like to say so. She'd already backed Gemma up about searching the man's room and was sure if she objected again the others would think she was a drag. Besides, even Gemma wasn't objecting this time and if the man was a thief they might find some valuable evidence in the bag.

She watched anxiously as Luigi unzipped the bag. He peered inside. 'It's swimming gear,' he said disappointedly. 'Look.'

They all turned to look as Luigi pulled a corner of a big bath towel out of the bag.

'And just what do you kids think you're doing snooping in my bag!' an angry voice demanded.

Justin had been too busy looking at the stuff in the bag to spot the man coming back in. Now he had caught them red-handed going through his bag. He looked extremely cross.

Turn to page 92.

Kelvin explained that he was filming the video for his latest release and had disguised himself and checked in the hotel under a false name so he wouldn't be recognised.

'My fans are great,' he said, 'but sometimes I need a bit of privacy.'

They could all understand that.

'Mind you, I'm glad you kids got suspicious and decided to tag onto me,' he grinned. 'Otherwise I might have been a goner! Anyway,' he put his hand in his pocket and took out an envelope. 'I'd like you all to accept these free tickets to my concert in Sydney as a reward. I've put a note to your folks in the envelope too, explaining that you'll be personally collected from your homes by my chauffeur, and taken home again after the show. OK?'

OK? It was brilliant! The children all crowded around him, all trying to say their thanks at once.

Kelvin looked a bit embarrassed. 'Hey, remember that without you lot there might not have been a concert!'

'In that case, can I ask you one more favour?'

Everyone turned to look at Charlie. What did she want?

'Sure. Fire away!'

'Can I have your autograph?'

The End

Uncle Peter went to answer it and came back a few minutes later looking very grim faced and followed by Constable Mitchell, the local police officer, and another policeman.

'We hear that you kids have been spending money a bit freely just lately,' said Constable Mitchell. 'Money that was stolen from a hotel safe in Perth a few weeks ago.'

The next few hours were a nightmare. They all had to go down to the police station and answer a lot of awkward questions. Over and over again, they had to repeat how they found the money to the police sergeant. Then they had to wait at the station while Uncle Peter, Aunt Carol, Charlie's dad and Stavros's parents were all questioned too.

It was ages before the police finally believed that they had nothing to do with the robbery and allowed them all home.

The grown-ups were furious. Gemma, Justin and Stavros were grounded for the entire summer holidays. Charlie's dad was so angry and upset with her that he booked them both on the next flight home. They left early the next morning.

Charlie choked back the tears as she looked out of the window of the plane. She had known it was wrong to spend the money, she should have spoken up instead of going along with the others. If only they had left the bag where it was, or told someone about it instead of lying she'd still be having a lovely holiday in Australia. As it was, she doubted if she'd ever see her cousins again and she knew it would be a long time before her father would trust her again. But, worst of all, she knew that she'd let Jesus down.

The End

Charlie didn't like the sound of either of these ideas.

'Don't you think you should tell your parents about your suspicions, Luigi, and leave it up to them to sort out?' she asked. 'If he is a thief then he could be dangerous. And if he isn't and we follow him he might see us and get annoyed.'

They all thought about it and agreed that what Charlie said made sense.

'You're right. My folks will stress out if I upset a guest,' Luigi nodded. 'I'll tell them about it tonight and see what they say. Meanwhile, let's forget about the Mystery Man for now and have a game of squash.'

'Hey, I thought we were showing Charlie around first,' said Gemma.

'Sorry, I forgot. Come on, Charlie, I'll give you a guided tour of the place and then me and Justin'll beat you and Gemma at squash!'

'In your dreams!' Gemma told him. 'We could lick you two with one hand tied behind our backs!'

Laughing and joking together, the four friends set off to show Charlie around the hotel.

Turn to page 96.

Aunt Carol was surprised to see them back from the beach so early. 'Have you got bored with sunbathing already, Charlie?'

'No, it's great!' Charlie told her. 'I could stop there all day!'

'We said we'd take her to the wildlife park. That'll be OK, won't it, Mum?' asked Gemma.

'Yes, of course, we've been there so many times I'm sure you could find your way around blindfolded!' smiled Aunt Carol. 'Are you going after lunch?'

'We were hoping to take a picnic and eat lunch there,' Justin told her.

'That's a lovely idea. There's plenty of cheese and cooked meat in the fridge. Just help yourselves,' said Aunt Carol.

'I'll go and raid the fridge at home too,' Stavros told them. 'Mum made some lamingtons yesterday and if we're lucky there might be some left.'

'What are lamingtons?' Charlie asked curiously. 'They sound like some sort of little animal!'

Gemma laughed. 'They're little sponge cakes covered in chocolate and dipped in coconut. You'll love them. They're delicious!'

'They sound it,' agreed Charlie.

'I've just thought – Rashida might be back by now.' Gemma dashed out of the kitchen. 'Hey, Stavros!' she shouted after their Greek friend who was now half-way down the drive. 'Call for Rashida and see if she wants to come. She might be in now!'

Stavros waved his hand in acknowledgement.

Turn to page 90.

'Maybe he's meeting someone in the sea. That'd be the perfect cover.' Justin glanced along the beach to see if anyone else was in sight. It was deserted.

'Let's go and sit over there. We can pretend we're sunbathing,' suggested Gemma. 'That way we can keep an eye on the man and see if anyone else comes along.'

'Well, we ended up coming down to the beach after all,' Charlie smiled as they all sat down on the sand.

'So we did,' Gemma grinned at her. 'I don't think you're going to get your game of squash today. Sorry.'

Charlie didn't mind. Following the Mystery Man to see if he was a thief was a lot more exciting than playing squash!

She scooped up a handful of sand and let it trickle through her fingers. It was soft and warm. Hard to believe that back at home they were in the middle of winter.

'Doesn't look like the guy is meeting anyone after all,' said Justin, looking over at the sea where the man was still swimming alone. He was now barely visible. Justin frowned worriedly. 'Hey, he's swimming a bit far out, isn't he? Doesn't he know he's supposed to keep within the flags? He'll get swept away by the currents if he isn't careful.'

They all turned to look at the man. He was very far out. Charlie saw that Gemma and Luigi were worried too.

Turn to next page.

'Why are you all so worried?' she asked. 'I'm sure the man will be OK. He's probably a very good swimmer.'

'He'd need to be, the currents are very strong here,' Gemma told her. 'A lot of tourists don't realise how strong they are and get dragged out beyond their depth.'

'And then there's the danger of sharks,' added Luigi. 'We haven't had any around here for a while but you never know when the next one's gonna turn up.'

'Sharks.' Charlie went pale and glanced nervously at the sea. 'Do you really have sharks in the sea around her?'

'We sure do,' Justin rose to his feet and peered over to the sea. The man was bobbing about and waving to them.

'See, he's OK. He's waving to us,' Charlie looked relieved.

The others looked grim.

'He's waving to tell us he needs help,' Gemma told her. 'I reckon he's out of his depth and the currents are too strong for him to make it back.'

'I'll go and get the life-saver,' Luigi sprinted off across the beach. Gemma and Justin waved back to the man and pointed to Luigi, trying to tell them that he was going for help.

Turn to page 94.

'I think we'd better call the police and let them know what's happened,' Aunt Carol said, walking over to the telephone on the kitchen wall. 'Have you still got the note you found, Charlie?'

'I think it's in my bag,' Charlie raced back to the garage where they had all left their beach bags, picked her bag up off the floor and rummaged through it. She was sure she'd put the note in there. Ah, here it was. She pulled out the crumpled piece of paper and ran back to the house with it.

Aunt Carol had already dialled the number.

'I've found the note!' Charlie told her. 'Will the police want it?'

'I should think they'll want whatever evidence they can get,' said Aunt Carol. 'Good day, Constable Mitchell, it's Carol Baxter here. My children and their friends have found a bagful of money . . . '

Constable Mitchell and another police officer came to question the children. They took away the bag of money and the note, praising them for their prompt action in telling Aunt Carol about finding the money.

Turn to next page.

Uncle Peter and Charlie's dad were very pleased too, when they heard about the events that evening. So were Stravros's parents. They all promised to take the children to see a film as a treat for being so honest.

Charlie was really pleased that she had spoken up about keeping the money. It had been hard, but she knew she had done the right thing and she was sure Jesus was pleased with her.

Constable Mitchell came around the next day to tell them that the money had been stolen from a hotel in Perth, along with a haul of jewellery. Evidently there was a gang of jewel thieves operating in hotels throughout Australia, robbing the guests of jewellery and raiding the hotel safes. The hotel manager at Perth had recognised the writing on the note as belonging to a barman who had disappeared recently. The police were circulating a description of the man and hoped to have him in for questioning soon.

Next day they all had a visit from the hotel manager from Perth. He was so pleased to get his money back he had flown over to thank the children personally. And as a reward he offered the four children and their families a free weekend at his hotel – including tickets for the flight. The children were all very excited. Especially Charlie. Her holiday in Australia looked like being even better than she'd dreamed!

The End

Tim came to see them later that afternoon. He seemed very amused about something.

'Did you catch the smugglers?' Justin asked anxiously.

'Smugglers!' he laughed. 'What an imagination you kids have got! Those men were loading stuff in the caves ready to shoot a video early tomorrow morning. And guess who's the star of the video?'

A video? So the crates had just contained props and equipment! Oh no, and they'd called the police and almost set the men's boat adrift! They all felt really stupid.

'Kelvin Starr!' Tim had got fed up waiting for an answer to his question.

'What?' Gemma looked at him blankly.

'Kelvin Starr. He's doing a tour of Australia and is staying at the Century Hotel for a few days. He wants to shoot the video for his next release on the beach.'

Charlie gaped at him. Kelvin Starr, the famous pop star! Staying here! And they'd almost wrecked his video!

The others were thinking the same thing.

'Oh no, I feel a right wally!' groaned Gemma, putting her hand to her forehead.

'Luckily, the men thought it was quite amusing,' Tim told them. 'They gave me one of these for each of you.' He handed them signed photographs of Kelvin Starr.

They were all delighted! A signed photograph of Kelvin Starr! Maybe they hadn't made such a mess of things on the beach, after all!

The End

Stavros returned half an hour later, with the promised lamingtons, some fruit and a pile of Vegemite sandwiches.

'Rashida'll be along in a few minutes,' he said. 'She's just got back from shopping with her mum.'

'Great!' Gemma was really pleased. Rashida was her best friend and she was sure Charlie would get on with her too.

She was right, Charlie and Rashida got on very well. It turned out that Rashida had an uncle who lived in England, and in fact owned a shop not far away from where Charlie lived!

'Mum and Dad are always saying we'll visit Uncle Ahmed one day,' she told Charlie. 'If we ever do I'll look you up!'

'That'd be ace!' Charlie smiled. 'I'll tell your uncle that I met you. I often pop into his shop if Nan's run out of anything, 'cos it's open late.'

Charlie and her father had lived with her grandparents since her mother died when she was very little. Nan was very absent-minded and was always running out of things like sugar and bread. Charlie couldn't wait to tell Mr Sharma that she had met his niece in Australia. She knew he would be delighted.

'Are you all ready then? The bus will be along in a few minutes,' Aunt Carol reminded them. She opened her purse and took out some money, handing a couple of dollars each to Justin, Gemma and Charlie. 'Here, you'll need a bit of money each. How about you two?' she asked Stavros and Rashida. 'Have you got enough money?'

Turn to next page.

They both assured her that they had. Then the children picked up their bags and set off to catch the bus.

Charlie thought the wildlife park was really beautiful. She gazed around in wonder at the colourful plants and birds. Then to her delight a couple of kangaroos bounded out of the bushes in front of them.

'They're really cute!' she exclaimed. 'Look, that one's just a baby!'

'We call baby kangaroos joeys,' Gemma told her. 'They are cute, aren't they?'

Charlie was puzzled about something. 'Don't kangaroos run wild any more?' she asked. 'Are they only kept in the wildlife parks?'

'Oh no, there's plenty of them in the bush,' Justin told her. 'And sometimes we see them in the countryside near the cities too.'

'Dad said a group of them came bounding onto the golf course last week, just as he was about to putt!' chuckled Stavros. 'He reckons he would have won the game if they hadn't put him off his shot!'

They all laughed, explaining to Charlie that Stavros's father had only just started to play golf and wasn't too good at it yet, so he used any excuse for his bad shots!

Turn to page 41.

Justin thought fast. 'We found it by the chair and were looking through it to see who it belonged to,' he lied.

'Don't lie to me, kid,' the man growled. 'You lot were hanging about here when I left so you must have known it was my bag.' He looked closely at Luigi. 'You're the kid whose parents run this place, aren't you? Well, let's see what they've got to say about you snooping around in guests' bags.'

Luigi looked worriedly at his friends. Now he was for it!

It turned out that the bearded man was none other than Kelvin Starr, the famous pop star. Kelvin was doing a tour of Australia and had booked in at the Century Hotel under a different name, and disguised himself, because he didn't want any of his fans besieging the hotel. He was so annoyed with the children for snooping in his bag that he checked out of the hotel immediately, threatening to complain to the chairman of the hotel group.

The four children couldn't believe that they actually mistook Kelvin Starr for a jewel thief and snooped in his bag!

Luigi's parents were extremely cross. They had lost a very important guest and when the chairman of the hotel group got to hear about it they could be in even more trouble. Luigi was grounded for the rest of the holidays. Gemma, Justin and Charlie knew they would be in trouble too, once they got home.

But whatever punishment their parents gave them couldn't be worse than blowing the chance of getting Kelvin Starr's autograph.

The End

'Get real! Someone might catch us! Anyway, my parents'd stress out if I snooped in a guest's bag,' said Luigi.

The others agreed that it would be wrong to snoop at his property so they all set off to follow the man.

Outside the hotel they looked around for him.

Charlie spotted him first. 'There he is, walking over to the car park.'

'Oh no, we should have guessed he had a car,' groaned Gemma. 'Now how are we going to follow him?'

However, the man suddenly stopped, turned and headed back into the hotel. He came back out with his bag.

'Thank goodness we didn't sneak a look in it. He'd have caught us right in the act!' gasped Justin.

They kept a careful distance behind the man, and to their surprise, he headed for a secluded stretch of the beach.

'Maybe he's meeting someone here to discuss secret plans,' Justin said.

'It looks to me like he's going for a swim,' Gemma told him. The man had now stopped and was pulling off his tee shirt. They watched as he opened up his bag and took out some goggles. Then he thrust his shirt into the bag, zipped it back up again and ran towards the sea.

The four friends looked at each other, what were they supposed to do now?

If they stay on the beach and keep an eye on the man, turn to page 85.

If they go back to the hotel, turn to page 52.

Within minutes a couple of life-savers were racing towards them on their beach buggy. They both jumped off and looked over at the sea. The man bobbed up in the water then a huge wave swept over him.

Charlie watched with bated breath as one of the life-savers dived into the sea, swimming through the turbulent waves towards the man. As he swam, his partner reeled out the line that was fixed to his belt.

'I hope he reaches him in time,' said Gemma anxiously.

'Let's pray that he does,' said Charlie.

To the other children's surprise she shut her eyes and started to pray. 'Please Jesus, help the life-saver rescue the man in the sea.'

Luigi joined her without hesitation. Gemma and Justin looked at each other awkwardly. They didn't normally pray. But Charlie seemed to think it was a perfectly normal thing to do. And the man was in danger. So was the life-saver. It looked as if only God could save them. Without further hesitation they closed their eyes and listened to Charlie.

'Can you kids give me a hand hauling them in?' shouted the second life-saver. His partner in the sea had reached the man and was now trying to bring him back. The four children immediately rushed to help the life-saver haul them both in on the line attached to his belt.

Turn to next page.

At last the man was safely on the beach. He was breathless and exhausted but safe.

'Thanks!' he gasped when he finally got his breath back. 'I thought I was a goner then.'

'You nearly were, mate,' the life-savers told him. 'Don't you know you're supposed to swim within the flags? If it weren't for these kids raising the alarm I don't think we'd have got to you in time.'

The man looked over at the four children and nodded. 'Thanks, kids!'

The children lowered their eyes and mumbled that they were glad to help. They couldn't look the guy in the face. You see, Luigi had been right, the guy was wearing a wig – and right now it was hanging half off!

They had to get away to discuss this. Making their excuses, they quickly left the beach.

'See, I told you he was wearing a wig!' Luigi said triumphantly as soon as they were out of earshot.

'Maybe he's a thief, after all,' said Gemma. 'What shall we do?'

Charlie had been quiet all the way back from the beach. She was thinking hard. Something about that man had seemed vaguely familiar. 'You know, I'm sure I've seen that man before,' she said slowly. 'But I can't think where.'

Turn to page 48.

Charlie thought the hotel was brilliant. She couldn't believe the size of it and all the facilities. It even offered a disco. After a strenuous game of squash, which had ended in a draw, they had popped into the hotel café for a milkshake.

Luigi telephoned them after tea, to tell them that he had mentioned the Mystery Man to his parents who had assured him that they knew the man and there was nothing to worry about. They were all relieved to hear that, and glad that they hadn't done anything silly like searching his room.

'Thank you for a wonderful day, Jesus,' Charlie prayed before she got into bed that night. 'And for giving me the chance to go on this brilliant holiday.'

The holiday passed too quickly. Most of the time they either went to the beach or the leisure centre. At the weekend, they all went to a wildlife park and Charlie was delighted when she was allowed to hold a cuddly koala. She took lots of photos of the animals there, to show her friends back home.

Luigi's parents had invited Charlie, her father, aunt, uncle and cousins to a farewell meal at their hotel that evening.

'Have you both enjoyed your stay here?' they asked.

'It's been brill!' Charlie told them. 'I wish we didn't have to go home tomorrow. I wish we could stay another week.'

Turn to page 75.